Sunglass Island

First Edition

PAGE PUBLISHING, INC.
New York, NY

First originally published by Page Publishing, Inc. 2019

ISBN 978-1-64424-880-5 (Paperback)
ISBN 978-1-64584-014-5 (Hardcover)
ISBN 978-1-64424-881-2 (Digital)

Printed in the United States of America

Sunglass Island

To [illegible], May you have fun on Sunglass Island! Alice Romanstine-Hall

ALICE ROMANSTINE-HALL

Have you ever been at the beach having the time of your life playing in the surf or building sandcastle when a big wave crashes over your head?

All at once you are blinded by the sunshine!

You look around for your sunglasses, but they are gone!

You cannot find them anywhere!

Where do the sunglasses go?

Does your family lose their sunglasses on your family vacations?

Our family does!

Where do the sunglasses go?

On the first day of our vacation, Trace was testing out his new boogie board and caught the perfect wave!

He came to shore holding his boogie board with both hands!

The sun was so bright.

Trace reached for his sunglasses in a squinting panic, and they were gone!

Where did Trace's sunglasses go?

On the second day of vacation, Ansley was jumping waves on her Jet Ski and turning circles! All of a sudden, the water became choppy, and a giant wave flipped her over!

Within a few seconds, she was back on her Jet Ski, but her sunglasses fell victim to the ocean!

Where did Ansley's sunglasses go?

On the third day of vacation, Elijah was building his sandcastle far from the shore to protect it from the waves!

When the castle was complete, Elijah went to rinse his hands, buckets, and shovels in the surf.

Oh, it happens so quick! When Elijah bent over, the waves swallowed his sunglasses into the ocean!

Where did Elijah's sunglasses go?

On the fourth day of vacation, Lila, Mackenzie, and Adalyn were taking an afternoon stroll on the beach. As they walked, they scanned the surf for sharks' teeth. Mackenzie spotted a rough patch of shells and possible sharks' teeth. She needed a closer look, so she moved her sunglasses to the top of her head. A group of pelicans were flying very low above the girls. When the girls looked up, Mackenzie's sunglasses slipped off her head! They were lost to the ocean!

Where did Mackenzie's sunglasses go?

On the fifth day of vacation, our whole family went on a boat adventure to explore!

The first island we visited was famous for monkeys, but we did not see any monkeys on Monkey Island. Do you see any monkeys?

The second island we visited was Shell Island known for giant conch shells! We each collected one shell.

The last island we visited was a mysterious island!
The island was not on the map or GPS!
We pulled closer to shore, and the island looked a little familiar.
We saw a game of volleyball on the beach and sunbathing.

SUNGLASS ISLAND HOTEL
SUNGLASS
SNOW CONES

SUNGLASS
SCHOOL
SUNGLASS ISLAND HOTEL
SUNGLASS
SNOW CONES
FOOD

We saw a small school, a snow cone shack, and even a church.

However, we did not see people!

As we pulled closer to the island, we saw sunglasses!

We discovered where all of our lost sunglasses had gone!

We discovered Sunglass Island on our boat adventure!

So if you lose your glasses in the water, please don't fret. They are now on Sunglass Island you can bet!

Sunglass Island is where all lost sunglasses go!

About the Author

Sunglass Island is a charming story that takes a peek into the life of lost sunglasses!

Inspired by her children and grandchildren who would spend endless hours playing in the waves at Edisto Beach, South Carolina, and her family exploring trips of the barrier islands, the story was created to provide them an exclusive perspective of what happened to their lost sunglasses.

The greatest role of her life is being a Mama and Nana! Being from a large family, she learned the importance of valuing everyone God places in their lives!

Over the years, she has created many stories specifically for her children!

Sunglass Island is one of their favorites!

It is her pleasure to share it with your family too!

CPSIA information can be obtained
at www.ICGtesting.com
Printed in the USA
LVHW070607050719
623172LV00003B/13/P